Pooh's Easter Egg Hunt

Disney's

Winnie the Pooh First Readers

Pooh Gets Stuck
Bounce, Tigger, Bounce!
Pooh's Pumpkin
Rabbit Gets Lost
Pooh's Honey Tree
Happy Birthday, Eeyore!
Pooh's Best Friend
Tiggers Hate to Lose
The Giving Bear
Pooh's Easter Egg Hunt
Eeyore Finds Friends
Pooh's Hero Party
Pooh's Surprise Basket
Pooh and the Storm That Sparkled

Disney's

A Winnie the Pooh First Reader

Pooh's Easter Egg Hunt

by Isabel Gaines

ILLUSTRATED BY Studio Orlando

NEW YORK

SPECIAL EDITION

First Edition

1 3 5 7 9 10 8 6 4 2

Library of Congress Catalog Card Number: 98-86077

ISBN: 0-7868-4352-7

For more Disney Press fun, visit www.DisneyBooks.com

Pooh's Easter Egg Hunt

"Happy Easter!" Winnie the Pooh called to his friends.

They were all at Rabbit's house

for his Easter egg hunt.

"All right, everybody," Rabbit said. "Whoever finds the most eggs wins. Get ready . . . get set . . . go!"

Pooh, Piglet, Roo, Tigger,

Eeyore, and Kanga

ran into the woods.

Pooh found a yellow egg

under some daffodils.

He put the egg in his basket.

Poor Pooh didn't know

his basket

had a hole in it.

The yellow egg slipped out

and fell onto the soft grass.

Piglet found the yellow egg.

"Lucky me!" he said.

Then Pooh found a purple egg

behind a rock.

He put the purple egg

in his basket.

Oops! This egg slipped out, too.

Roo found the purple egg.

"Oh, goody!" he cried.

"Purple's my favorite color!"

Pooh found a green egg in a tree,

and put it in his basket.

He didn't see it fall back out.

Tigger found the green egg.

"Hoo-hoo-hoo!" Tigger cried.

"I'm on my way to winning!"

Next Pooh found a red egg . . .

. . . that slipped through the hole

and into a clump of thistle.

Eeyore found the red egg.

"Surprise," he mumbled.

"I found an Easter egg."

On the side of a grassy hill,

Pooh found a blue egg.

“How pretty.”

Pooh continued up the hill—

as the egg rolled down it.

Kanga found Pooh's blue egg

lodged against a log.

Finally, Rabbit shouted, "Time's up!"

Everyone gathered around.

"Let's see who won," Rabbit said.

Piglet, Roo, Tigger, Eeyore,

and Kanga showed their Easter eggs.

Pooh looked inside his empty basket.

“My eggs seem to be hiding again,”

he said.

Piglet looked at Pooh's basket.
"I think I know where," Piglet said,
poking his hand through the hole.

"You can have my yellow egg," said Piglet. "It was probably your egg before it was mine."

"Thank you, Piglet," said Pooh.

"You can have my purple egg,
too," said Roo.

“Here, Buddy Bear,” said Tigger.
“Tiggers only like to win
fair and square.”

“Too good to be true,” muttered Eeyore, giving Pooh his red egg.

“And here’s my blue egg,” Kanga said.

"You're the winner, Pooh!"

Rabbit said.

"You win an Easter feast."

"Is there enough food
for my friends
to eat, too?" Pooh asked.

"I could make more,"

Rabbit said.

"Is there enough honey?" asked Pooh.

"There's plenty of honey," said Rabbit.

"Then let's eat!" said Pooh.

Everyone had a wonderful time.
Pooh enjoyed the food—
especially the honey!

Can you match the words with the pictures?

Kanga

basket

daffodil

purple

green

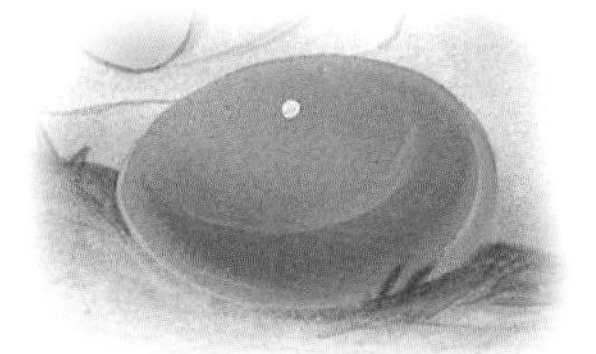

Fill in the missing letters.

P_oh

h_le

re_

_og

_oo

Join the Pooh Friendship Club!

A wonder-filled year of friendly activities and interactive fun for your child!

The fun starts with:

- Clubhouse play kit
- Exclusive club T-shirt
- The first issue of "Pooh News"
- Toys, stickers and gifts from Pooh

The fun goes on with:

- Quarterly issues of "Pooh News" each with special surprises
- Birthday and Friendship Day cards from Pooh
- And more!

Join now and also get a colorful, collectible Pooh art print

Yearly membership costs just $25 plus 15 Hunny Pot Points. (Look for Hunny Pot Points 3 on Pooh products.)

To join, send check or money order and Hunny Pot Points to:

Pooh Friendship Club
P.O. Box 1723
Minneapolis, MN 55440-1723

Please include the following information: Parent name, child name, complete address, phone number, sex (M/F), child's birthday, and child's T-shirt size (S, M, L)
(CA and MN residents add applicable sales tax.)

Call toll-free for more information
1-888-FRNDCLB

Kit materials not intended for children under 3 years of age. Kit materials subject to change without notice. Please allow 8-10 weeks for delivery. Offer expires 6/30/99. Offer good while supplies last. Please do not send cash. Void where restricted or prohibited by law. Quantities may be limited. Disney is not liable for correspondence, requests, or orders delayed, illegible, lost or stolen in the mail. Offer valid in the U.S. and Canada only. ©Disney. Based on the "Winnie the Pooh" works, copyright A.A. Milne and E.H. Shepard.

Fun for kids ages 3-8!

Pooh Friendship Club